Special thanks to Linda Chapman
To Mia Bevis, Harriet Farley and Elissa
Cockayne – you would all make
brilliant Secret Princesses!

ORCHARD BOOKS

First published in Great Britain in 2016 by The Watts Publishing Group

3 5 7 9 10 8 6 4

A CIP catalogue record for this book
is available from the British Library.

ISBN 978 1 40833 610 6

Printed and bound in Great Britain by Clays Ltd, St Ives plc

The paper and board used in this book are made from wood from responsible sources.

Orchard Books
An imprint of
Hachette Children's Group
Part of The Watts Publishing Group Limited
Carmelite House
50 Victoria Embankment
London EC4Y 0DZ

An Hachette UK Company
www.hachette.co.uk
www.hachettechildrens.co.uk

Series created by Hothouse Fiction
www.hothousefiction.com

Dolphin
Adventure

ROSIE BANKS

Wishing Star Palace

The Secret Princess Promise

"I promise that I will be kind and brave,

Using my magic to help and save,

Granting wishes and doing my best,

To make people smile and bring happiness."

CONTENTS

Chapter One: An Unexpected Trip   11

Chapter Two: A Special Ceremony   27

Chapter Three: Emily   41

Chapter Four: Rain, Rain Go Away   59

Chapter Five: Sun and Fun   77

Chapter Six: A Dream Come True   95

CHAPTER ONE

An Unexpected Trip

"This way, please!" the tour guide called, leading the class through the dark tunnels of the aquarium. "In here you'll see a wonderful display of tropical fish."

Mia Thompson tucked her long blonde hair behind her ears and followed the rest of her class into the next room. One wall had a large pane of glass that reached from the

 11

floor all the way up to the ceiling. On the other side of the glass, tiny blue, yellow and green fish were swooping around in shoals while larger orange fish weaved between the rocks and seaweed.

"So, who can tell me what fish eat?" the guide asked.

"Fish food!" one of the boys in Mia's class called out.

Everyone giggled.

The guide smiled. "Well, yes, but what *is* fish food in the wild?"

Mia knew the answer was plankton – she knew lots of facts about animals and sea creatures – but she was too shy to put up her hand.

"The little fish eat plankton," said
the guide when no one else answered.
"Plankton are teeny, tiny creatures that
float in the water."

Mia went closer to the glass. For a
moment, she imagined being a mermaid,
swimming among all the wonderful fish.
She half turned to tell her best friend,
Charlotte, what she was thinking, before
she realised that Charlotte wasn't there.
Charlotte had moved to America with
her family a few weeks ago. Mia felt a pang
of sadness in her heart. She and Charlotte
had been best friends ever since they
were little and they had always done
everything together.

We still get to do some things together, though, she thought. Touching the golden necklace that was hidden under her school jumper, Mia smiled as she remembered the incredible secret she and Charlotte shared. Both girls had matching necklaces with a pendant in the shape of half a heart. They had been given to them by their grown-up friend, Alice. When Charlotte had moved away, the girls had both wished to see each other – and something absolutely amazing had happened. The necklaces had whisked both girls away to a gorgeous palace high up in the clouds! Alice had met them there and told them she was a Secret Princess – someone who could magically grant wishes.

Mia and Charlotte had been even more astonished when Alice had told them that they had the potential to become Secret Princesses, too!

Suddenly, Mia felt a tingle run across her skin. It was coming from her necklace! Dropping away from her class as they followed the guide towards the next display, she slipped back into the tunnel and pulled the necklace out.

Warm light sparkled off it, lighting up the dim tunnel. Mia's heart skipped a beat. If her necklace was

glowing, it meant she was going to see Charlotte. Maybe they'd even get to grant another wish!

She closed her fingers around the pendant. *I wish I could see Charlotte,* she thought. Suddenly, the world seemed to drop away and she was spinning and tumbling through the air. Luckily, no time passed in their real lives while they were on a Secret Princess adventure, so no one would notice that she was gone.

Mia's feet hit soft grass and her eyes blinked open. She was standing in a beautiful garden filled with rose bushes, and her school clothes had changed into a gorgeous golden dress with a full skirt.

She put her hand up and felt a tiara
nestling in her blonde hair. Wisps of fluffy
white cloud were floating around the garden
and lollipops and candyfloss hung from
the branches of the trees. Mia ran to an
archway of roses and looked through.

"Wishing Star Palace!" she breathed in excitement, as she saw the grand white palace with its four turrets twisting up into the sky. It looked beautiful from a distance but Mia knew that if she got closer she would see that the paint was peeling, there were tiles missing from the turrets and that the panes of glass in the heart-shaped windows were cracked. She and Charlotte were determined to make it beautiful again!

"Mia! Mia!"

Swinging round, Mia saw Charlotte running towards her, her brown curls bouncing on her shoulders and a delighted smile on her freckly face.

She was wearing a light pink princess dress with roses on the skirt, and like Mia she had her pendant around her neck and a tiara in her hair.

With a squeal of joy, Mia raced over
to her best friend. They hugged each
other tightly.

"Oh, wow! I can't believe we're back!"
said Charlotte, letting go of Mia and
jumping up and down with excitement.
"I almost thought I'd dreamt it."

"We didn't dream it," said Mia, looking
at the half-heart pendant. "The diamond
proves it really happened!"

When Alice had first given them their
necklaces, the half-hearts had been pure
gold, but after they granted a girl named
Olivia's wish to have a brilliant birthday
party, a diamond had appeared in each of
their pendants. Alice had explained that

if they helped three more people, they'd get three more diamonds. Once they had them all, their plain tiaras would turn into the beautiful jewelled tiaras that all Secret Princesses wore. Even more importantly, they would be one step closer to becoming fully fledged Secret Princesses!

"Should we go to the palace and see if we can find Alice?" asked Mia, excitement bubbling through her.

Holding hands, they ran through the arch. As they got closer to the palace, Charlotte pointed upwards. Three of the turrets had missing tiles, but one of the turrets looked like new, its golden tiles glittering in the sunshine.

"Look!" said Charlotte. "It's the turret that got mended when we made Olivia's wish come true."

Mia nodded proudly. "I hope we can repair more of Wishing Star Palace by granting someone else's wish."

"I bet we will," said Charlotte. "Oh, I can't wait to have another adventure!" Her brown eyes sparkled.

Mia's tummy fluttered nervously. "But what if we meet Princess Poison again?"

Princess Poison was the reason Wishing Star Palace was crumbling. She was once a Secret Princess herself, but now she used her magic to spoil wishes. Every time she succeeded, she grew more powerful and

Wishing Star Palace crumbled a bit more. The only way to repair the palace was by granting wishes, but Princess Poison was doing everything she could to make sure that didn't happen.

Mia imagined tall, thin Princess Poison with her cold green eyes and her long black hair with its ice-blonde streak and shuddered. After they'd refused to join her and her horrid servant, Hex, Princess Poison had sworn to stop Mia and Charlotte from granting any more wishes.

Charlotte shrugged. "Who cares if we see Princess Poison? We'll beat her!"

Mia smiled and squeezed her best friend's hand tightly.

"Girls! Up here!"

"It's Alice!" said

Mia, spotting their

friend waving from

one of the palace's

heart-shaped

windows.

Alice looked as cool as ever. Her strawberry-blonde hair had red streaks in it and she was wearing her gorgeous red princess dress.

"Hi, Alice!" Charlotte called, waving up at her.

"Hurry up!" Alice said. "The ceremony's about to start!"

"What ceremony?" called Mia.

Alice smiled. "Come inside and find out!"

CHAPTER TWO

A Special Ceremony

As Mia and Charlotte reached the palace doors, Alice came down to greet them. "Welcome back!" she said, giving them both a hug.

Alice's red dress had a full skirt and her tiara was studed with shining diamonds. She wore a gold necklace around her neck with a pendant shaped like a musical note.

Alice had once been the girls' babysitter, but now she was a pop star and travelled all over the world – when she wasn't at Wishing Star Palace!

Mia thought how surprised Alice's fans would be if they knew that she was also a Secret Princess!

"You're just in time for the Princess Ceremony," Alice said. "Evie has finished all her training and is about to become a full Secret Princess! This might be your only chance to see the ceremony. Apart from Evie, you two are the only trainees left."

"Why?" asked Charlotte.

Alice's face fell and her voice grew serious. "Princess Poison has caused so

much trouble that she's scared all the other
trainees away. That's why we're so pleased
to have you. Because you girls have each
other, you can stand up to Princess Poison!"

Mia glanced at her necklace in delight.
On their first visit to Wishing Star Palace,
Mia and Charlotte had discovered that they
had the potential to be a very rare kind
of Secret Princess – Friendship Princesses!
Friendship Princesses came in pairs and
their magic was extra strong because they
always worked together. Mia still couldn't
believe she got to be a princess with her
very best friend!

Just then a clock sounded inside the
palace. Alice gasped, taking their hands.

"The ceremony's about to start and we need your help. Come on!" she said.

"What do we have to do?" Mia asked.

But Alice didn't reply. She was too busy hurrying them into a large hall with a domed roof. It would once have been very grand but the pillars were crumbling and there were cracks in the walls. Garlands of

freshly picked pink, lilac and white flowers had been hung around the room to hide the damage. There was a small stage with a throne, also decorated with flowers.

A young princess in a grass-green dress trimmed with petals was sitting on the throne and a group of chattering Secret Princesses sat around it in a semicircle.

Mia gazed around, trying to see their pendants. Secret Princesses were all kind, helpful and brave, but they also each had their own special talents. Alice's pendant was a musical note because she was so good at singing. Mia spotted a princess with deep red hair piled up on top of her head – it was Princess Sylvie. She had a cupcake pendant because she was very good at baking. But none of the Secret Princesses had matching pendants like Mia and Charlotte's. As she and Charlotte sat down, Mia heard one princess whisper, "Look! It's the new Friendship Princess trainees!"

An older Secret Princess walked onto the stage and the chattering stopped.

"That's Princess Anna," whispered Alice.

Princess Anna had grey hair coiled in a bun and a kindly face with sparkling green eyes. Her dress was sky blue with golden embroidery, and she had an owl pendant. Mia guessed that it meant she was very wise.

"Welcome everyone," Princess Anna said. "I'm delighted that you are all here today for Evie's Princess Ceremony. She has helped many people and thoroughly earned the right to become a Secret Princess."

She smiled warmly at the girl sitting on the throne. "Evie, by helping people you have earned everything you need to become a true Secret Princess.

You have your princess tiara, shoes, bracelet, cloak and ring. Now there is just one thing left for you to be given, the most  important item of all – your own magic wand." She took a slim silver wand out of a pocket in her dress and held it up.

She turned to the room and looked at the rest of the princesses. "Our tradition is for our newest trainee princess to present the wand. Today I am happy to say we have not one, but *two* new trainee princesses with us." Her gaze fell on Charlotte and Mia and she smiled. "Charlotte and Mia, please would you come up to the stage."

Charlotte jumped eagerly to her feet and hurried to the front. Mia followed more slowly. She could feel her cheeks blushing as all the princesses looked at her. As she reached the stage, Princess Anna's eyes caught hers. They were so kindly that Mia felt some of her nervousness slip away.

Princess Anna handed them the wand.

"Evie, are you ready to make your Secret Princess Promise?" she asked.

Evie's eyes shone with excitement. "Yes, I am." She took a deep breath and recited:

"I promise that I will be kind and brave,
Using my magic to help and save,
Granting wishes and doing my best,
To make people smile and bring happiness."

Princess Anna smiled. "Well done, my dear." Turning to Mia and Charlotte, she said, "Now, please give Princess Evie her wand, girls."

As they handed Princess Evie the wand,

it began to glow, and suddenly a silver flower symbol appeared at one end of it.

Light radiated outwards from the flower until everything about Evie – her dress, her tiara, and her necklace – shone with sparkling light.

Evie stood up and waved her wand joyfully as thousands of rose petals exploded out of the tip. Shooting into the air, the petals floated down, filling the whole Grand Hall with the scent of roses.

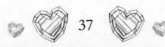

Charlotte twirled round, catching them
with her hands as the other princesses
jumped up from their chairs to hug and
congratulate the newest Secret Princess.

Mia edged back shyly and felt a hand
gently squeeze her arm. She turned and saw
Alice beside her. "One day that will be you
and Charlotte," said Alice.

"Oh, I hope so," breathed Mia. There
was nothing she wanted more than to be a
Secret Princess.

Everyone was smiling and laughing and
then suddenly the ends of everyone's wands
started glowing like fairy lights.

"Why are all the wands shining?" Mia
whispered. "Is it part of the ceremony?"

"No, they're glowing because someone needs help," said Alice. "Are you two ready for another adventure?"

"Definitely," said Charlotte.

"But shouldn't one of you go instead?" asked Mia. "You're all proper Secret Princesses – we're just trainees."

"All the more reason why you two should go. We need you to become Secret Princesses as quickly as possible, and that will only happen if you grant lots of wishes." Alice set off for the door. "Come quickly!" she called over her shoulder. "We need to get to the Mirror Room as fast as we can!"

CHAPTER THREE
Emily

"Good luck! Good luck!" the other Secret Princesses called as Mia and Charlotte hurried out of the Grand Hall. Mia's heart was beating fast. She and Charlotte were about to go on another adventure!

The Mirror Room was up a winding staircase at the top of one of the turrets. It was a small, circular room with nothing

inside it apart from a full-length oval mirror
in a tarnished frame. The surface of the
mirror swirled with golden light. Charlotte
and Mia went over to the Magic Mirror
and touched the surface together. A flash of
light ran across the glass and then a rhyme
appeared. Charlotte read it out:

"Your magic training is underway.
Someone needs your help today.
Each wish you grant, a diamond
you will own –
Four will give your your princess crown!"

The mirror's surface swirled with light
again. After a few seconds, it cleared to

 42

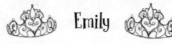

show a young girl sitting on a beach staring anxiously out at the sea. She had red hair tied in two plaits. Another rhyme appeared beneath the image:

A wish needs granting, adventures await.
Call Emily's name, don't hesitate!

"I wonder what Emily's wish is," said Charlotte.

"You'll soon find out," Alice replied, with a big smile. "Do you need me to come with you or do you want to go on your own this time?"

Mia wanted to ask Alice to come but she knew Secret Princesses had to be brave, so she forced herself to smile. "We'll be OK, won't we, Charlotte?"

"Absolutely," said Charlotte. "After all, we've got each other."

Their eyes met and Mia felt a new wave of confidence surge through her. As long as she and Charlotte were together, everything would be fine.

Alice nodded approvingly. "Just remember to watch out for Princess Poison."

"It's Princess Poison who'd better watch out for us!" said Charlotte determinedly. "We're going to help Emily and nothing will stop us!" She and Mia held hands and Charlotte counted down. "Three … two … one …"

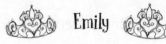

Emily

"*Emily!*" they both cried, touching the mirror at the same time. The light in the mirror began to swirl again, this time in a tunnel-like shape.

"Wheeee!" cried Charlotte as they were sucked inside the tunnel.

Mia's skin tingled all over. She felt like she was on the biggest water flume ever, with swirling light whooshing them along instead of water. They went faster and faster and finally flew out to land in a heap on soft golden sand. They were at the beach!

Mia heard the sound of the waves and felt the warmth of the sun's rays on her arms and face. No one seemed to have noticed them arrive, but that was all part of Secret Princess magic.

"We've got swimsuits on!" Charlotte said.

Glancing down, Mia realised their princess dresses had transformed into pretty swimsuits. Hers was turquoise blue with white seahorses an a ruffled skirt and Charlotte's had shorts and a purple polka-dot pattern on the top.

Charlotte jumped to her feet. "This is so cool!" she said, looking around at the sparkling sea and the golden sand. "It's like being on holiday."

"But we've got a job to do!" Mia said,
with a smile. "Where's Emily?"

Charlotte scanned the beach. "There she
is!" she said, spotting the little girl from the
Magic Mirror.

"Let's go and talk to her," said Mia. They
both hurried over.

Just as they got near to the little girl,

a lady called out from the water. "Come on, Em," the girls heard her say. "Why don't you come and play with Daddy, me and Sam in the water? It's so much fun."

"I don't want to." The girl shook her head. "Please don't make me, Mummy."

Her mum sighed. "OK, stay there for a bit longer then. We'll get out soon and then we'll all go and get an ice cream. I'll keep an eye on you from the water." She turned back to the sea, where a man and a boy were playing with a beach ball.

Mia watched as Emily picked up a bucket and spade and started to play miserably with the sand. Mia and Charlotte went over and sat down near her.

"Hi," said Charlotte, smiling at the younger girl.

Emily gave her a small smile back. "Hi."

"Are you OK?" Mia asked. Normally, she was shy about talking to people she didn't know, but Emily looked so sad she didn't feel nervous. "You don't look very happy."

"I'm not." Emily edged a bit closer. "I don't like being at the beach," she confessed.

"Why not?" Charlotte asked curiously. "The seaside is really fun!"

Emily shivered. "I don't like the sea. When I was swimming in it last year I got stung by a jellyfish. It really hurt."

"You poor thing," said Mia kindly. "It must have been horrible."

Emily's eyes filled with tears. "It was. Whenever I go near the sea now I think about that jellyfish. I really wish I wasn't scared of the sea."

Charlotte and Mia swapped looks. *So that was Emily's wish!* Mia thought. She glanced down at her pendant. As soon as it started to glow they would be able to grant three wishes to try and help Emily. But they

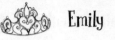

couldn't just make a big wish and take away her fear of the sea. Their necklaces' magic wasn't powerful enough. They had to think of three small wishes that might help.

Emily picked up her spade again and started digging unhappily in the sand. It gave Mia an idea. Maybe they could cheer Emily up and show her the seaside could be fun in other ways. "Shall we build a sandcastle together?" she said.

"Oh, yes!" said Charlotte. "It'll be fun."

Emily's eyes lit up. "I'd like that. We could decorate it with shells."

"And have a moat," said Charlotte.

"And make some flags out of lollipop sticks and seaweed," suggested Mia.

"Oh, yes!" said Emily, jumping up excitedly. "What are your names?"

"I'm Charlotte and this is Mia," Charlotte told her.

"My name's Emily," Emily said.

Mia only just stopped herself from saying, "*We know.*"

The girls started to make the sandcastle.

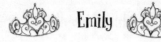

Mia loved drawing and making things, so while the others emptied out buckets of sand she started sculpting elegant towers and turrets. Then Emily collected some shells and bits of seaweed to decorate it while Charlotte dug a moat.

It was great fun. Emily still wouldn't go near the water but she seemed happier.

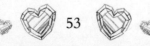

"Let's make some dolphins to put in the moat," said Mia.

She showed Emily how to gather up sand and shape it into a dolphin with a fin and a tail. Then she used a twig to draw in eyes and a smiling mouth.

Emily beamed. "Can we make some more? I love dolphins!"

"Me, too," said Mia. "I've got a poster of dolphins on my bedroom wall."

"I've got a dolphin necklace," said Emily. "I'd love to swim with dolphins, if it didn't mean going in the sea."

"Dolphins would chase away any jellyfish," Mia told her. "I saw it on a nature programme once."

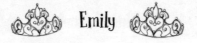

"I'd like to ride a dolphin and leap out of the water!" said Charlotte, doing a ballet jump in the air.

"You're really good at that," said Emily. "Will you teach me?"

So Charlotte started to teach Emily how to do a *jete* ballet jump. Emily fell over lots of times but she didn't seem to mind.

Maybe we'll be able to persuade her to come and play in the water with us, thought Mia. *She's looking much happier already.*

She picked up Emily's bucket. "Emily, why don't we get some water for the moat?"

Emily followed her to the water's edge but wouldn't actually go in the water. Mia filled the bucket and they carried it carefully back up to the sandcastle.

She had just lifted the bucket up to pour it in the moat when a small man came running past her. He was wearing flowery orange swimming shorts and had a very round tummy. He stumbled and bumped into Mia. "Whoops!" he said, as Mia dropped the bucket of water. The water

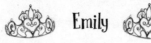

splashed everywhere and the bucket fell
onto the sandcastle! The turrets and towers
collapsed and the dolphins became a pile of
mushy sand.

"Oh, no! Our castle is ruined!" Emily
cried in dismay.

Mia swung round. The man had black beady eyes and a large bulbous nose.

"Hex!" Mia exclaimed. It was Princess Poison's servant!

Hex gave a mean chortle, grabbed Emily's bucket and ran away as fast as his legs could carry him.

"Hey! Give that back!" cried Mia.

"After him!" Charlotte exclaimed and, jumping over the ruined castle, she charged after the tubby little man.

CHAPTER FOUR
Rain, Rain Go Away

Mia raced after Charlotte and Hex. They jumped over people's legs, dodged around parasols and ducked to avoid Frisbees. Glancing back, Mia saw Emily, dripping wet and standing by the sandcastle staring in astonishment. Part of her wanted to go back and comfort the little girl, but she couldn't let Charlotte chase Hex on her own.

Charlotte was just reaching out to grab
Hex when he swerved sideways and crashed
into an ice cream seller. Ice cream cones
and ice lollies flew into the air. The poor
ice cream seller was knocked to the ground.
Hex scrambled over him, threw Emily's

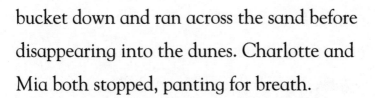

bucket down and ran across the sand before
disappearing into the dunes. Charlotte and
Mia both stopped, panting for breath.

"What just happened?" stammered the ice
cream seller.

Charlotte and Mia helped him stand up.
"Someone ran into you," said Charlotte.
"He's gone now."

"My ice creams," said the man in dismay,
looking around at all the cones scattered on
the sand.

"The ice lollies are still OK," said Mia.
She started to pick them up and wipe the
sand off the packets. Charlotte helped,
and soon they were back in the freezer
compartment. The cones that had been

on display were ruined, but luckily the ice cream seller had more in the cart.

"Thanks for your help, girls," he said, when everything was back to normal. "Have an ice lolly."

Mia chose a rocket lolly and Charlotte selected a cola-flavoured one. "Could we have one for our friend too, please?" asked Charlotte.

"Of course," he said.

The girls chose a strawberry split for Emily and walked back along the beach. "I can't believe Hex did that," said Charlotte crossly. "That was so mean."

"If he's here, that means Princess Poison must be nearby too," said Mia anxiously.

"We'd better keep our eyes peeled."

"Emily was having so much fun," said Charlotte. "I hope she's not too upset about the sandcastle."

But when they got back they found Emily was in tears. "Our sandcastle is completely ruined," she sobbed.

"Don't worry," said Charlotte, giving her a hug. "We've got you an ice lolly."

"We got your bucket back, too, so we can build it again," added Mia.

"But it'll take ages," said Emily. She licked the ice lolly sadly. "I hate the sea. It ruined our sandcastle. It ruins everything."

Mia felt a warmth on her chest and glanced down. Her pendant was glowing

with a soft light. Charlotte's was glowing too. Her fingers closed on the half-heart and she met Mia's eyes. "We could fix it," she said softly to Mia.

Mia nodded, guessing what her friend was thinking. They could use one of their wishes!

She and Charlotte fitted their pendants together. "We wish Emily could have the best sandcastle ever!" said Charlotte.

Rain, Rain Go Away

The pile of sand that had once been the ruined sandcastle started to glitter and glow and then, in the blink of an eye, it transformed into an amazing sandcastle that looked just like Wishing Star Palace! The turrets were decorated with white and pink shells, there were heart-shaped windows and even tiny sand roses around the doorway.

Emily gaped. "But… but… *how?*" she stammered. "How did you do that?"

"With magic," Mia said, taking Emily's hand. "Charlotte and I have a secret. You mustn't tell anyone, but we can make wishes come true. We're a bit like fairy godmothers."

65

"My big brother says that magic isn't real," Emily said.

"Well, he's wrong," said Charlotte, with a big grin.

"But our magic has to be a secret," said Mia. "No one else can know about it, and nobody will notice. Just you and us. OK?"

Emily nodded, her eyes as wide as saucers.

"We don't need magic to have fun here on the beach, though," said Charlotte. "Why don't we play by the rock pools?"

"Will I have to go in the water?" Emily asked nervously.

"Not if you don't want to," Mia assured her. "Come on! It will be fun!"

They left the castle and went closer to

the sea. Between the rocks were glittering little pools.

Mia crouched down and started poking around in one. "There are lots of things to see in here. Look!"

Emily and Charlotte joined her.

Mia pointed to a black object in amongst the shallow water. "It's a mermaid's purse!"

"Really?" Emily said.

Mia smiled. "Well, that's what my dad always calls them. They're actually little pouches that have stingray eggs in." She gently lifted it up and peered inside. "This one's empty, so it must have hatched."

A crab shuffled sideways along the sandy bottom of the pool. "That's a hermit crab.

They don't grow their own shells but find empty shells to live in. When they grow too big they have to find a new one."

"I can walk like a crab," said Charlotte. "Look!" She did a backwards walkover, landed in a crab position and walked sideways along the sand. "I'm a crab and I'm coming to get you, Emily!"

Emily giggled and ran a little way off.

Mia glanced back at their sandcastle and saw a tall, thin figure scowling at it. It was a woman in a green bathing suit that looked as if it was made of snakeskin, with a beach bag over her shoulder. Her long hair was black apart from an icy-blonde streak at the front, and her cold green eyes glittered nastily. Mia's heart turned a somersault.

"Look, Charlotte!" Mia squeaked. "It's Princess Poison!"

Charlotte jumped up from her crab position. "Emily, we're just popping back to the sandcastle for a moment," she called.

"OK," said Emily, who was busy inspecting a nearby rock pool.

Dolphin Adventure

Charlotte marched across the sand with Mia running after her.

Princess Poison gave a cruel smile.

"What are you doing here?" Charlotte demanded.

"I would have thought that was obvious," Princess Poison sneered. "I'm here to spoil Emily's wish." She sniggered. "You Secret Princesses aren't the only ones with a magic mirror." She pulled a shiny

70

green compact out of her beach bag and
showed them the mirror inside. "This lets
me spy on you. Whenever you try to grant
someone's wish, I'm going to be there to
spoil it." Her expression hardened. "I told
you that you'd regret making an enemy of
me. Why don't you just
give up and go away?"

Charlotte lifted her
chin defiantly. "We're
not going anywhere."

"No way," said Mia,
bravely.

"You foolish girls!"
Princess Poison said,
with a harsh laugh.

She placed her foot on one of the turrets of the sandcastle and squashed it flat. She smirked. "Oh, dear. Your precious sandcastle is crumbling, just like the real Wishing Star Palace! Soon it will vanish and I shall build a new palace in its place – Poison Palace!"

"That won't happen!" Charlotte exclaimed. "Every wish we grant is making Wishing Star Palace stronger."

"But what if you don't grant any more wishes?" said Princess Poison. "Poor Emily. She's never going to like the seaside. Not while I'm here!"

She suddenly pulled a green wand out of her beach bag, pointed it at the sky and hissed out a curse.

**"Wind whip up, raindrops fall down,
Chase smiles away, make everyone frown."**

The sky started to darken.
A wind blew up and cold
raindrops started to fall. "Oh,
what a shame. The day is
ruined for everybody."
Princess Poison smirked.

Clicking her fingers, she conjured up a
giant green umbrella. Then, giving the girls
a triumphant smile, she sauntered down
the beach past all the families who were
frantically starting to pack away all their
beach things.

The rain began to fall even harder, the cold drops making the girls shiver and quickly soaking their bathing suits. Emily came running back from the rock pools just as her mum, dad and brother came hurrying out of the sea. They were shivering and rubbing their arms.

"I don't know where this bad weather's come from," said Emily's dad. "We'd better grab our stuff and go."

"I'll get our towels," shouted Sam, Emily's older brother.

"Come on, Em," said Emily's mum. "Say goodbye to your new friends. Maybe you'll see them another day."

"Bye," Emily said sadly, waving to Mia

and Charlotte as she followed her parents.

Mia looked worriedly at Charlotte. "We can't let her go." If Emily left the beach, they wouldn't be able to grant her wish and Princess Poison would have won. They couldn't let that happen!

"We have to do something," said Charlotte. "What about making another wish?"

Mia glanced down at her necklace. It was still glowing, but the glow had faded slightly. "Do we have enough magic to change the weather?"

Charlotte picked up her pendant and held it up. "There's only one way to find out!"

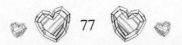

CHAPTER FIVE
Sun and Fun

Mia and Charlotte touched their pendants together. "It's your turn to make a wish, Mia," Charlotte whispered.

Mia thought carefully. She didn't want to use up a wish only for Princess Poison to immediately make it rain again and ruin their plans. What should she say? "We wish the wind and rain would go and the sun would shine brightly for the rest of the day!" she said finally.

There was a flash of light and the wind dropped instantly. The rain stopped, the clouds parted and a beautiful rainbow shimmered in the sunlight. Everyone on the beach looked up at the sky and laughed.

"It's sunny again!" they cried in delight.

People started opening up deckchairs and putting parasols back in the sand. Looking around, Mia spotted Emily's family putting their towels back out on the beach. Emily saw Mia and Charlotte and ran over.

"Now the weather's nice again, Mummy and Daddy said we can stay after all. Can we go back to the rock pools?"

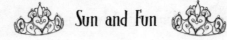

"Of course!" said Mia, glad that Emily was happy to stay on the beach. She glanced at her necklace. It was glowing very faintly now. They only had one more wish to use. *We'll have to use it wisely,* she thought.

Mia hurried after Charlotte and Emily as they raced back to the rock pools. They all crouched down and started poking around.

"Look," said Mia, pointing out some tiny darting fish. "I think they're sticklebacks." She lifted up some seaweed and found a small starfish underneath. She held it up and showed Emily the way the little tiny tubes on its underside wriggled. "Starfish move by wriggling all those little feet."

Mia carefully put it back in the pool.

"You know lots about sea creatures,"
Emily said, impressed.

"Mia knows lots about animals," said
Charlotte. She grinned. "But I know about
sea creatures too! Which fish is famous?"

"I don't know," said Emily. "Which one?"

Charlotte grinned. "The *starfish!*"

Emily giggled.

They carried on exploring the rock pools with Charlotte telling more silly jokes but, after a while, they all got very hot. "Let's go for a walk near the water to cool down," said Mia. *Maybe we can persuade Emily to paddle in the sea!* she thought happily.

They climbed over the rocks to the flat, damp sand at the edge of the water. "Let's go and see what's going on over there," said Charlotte, pointing to a quiet stretch of beach where there were only a couple of fishermen with a dinghy.

Emily ran to tell her mum what she was doing and then they all walked along the sand towards the boat. Emily kept away from the waves but Charlotte and Mia paddled. "Why don't you come in?" Charlotte urged Emily. "The water's lovely and cool."

"Um …" Emily hesitated.

"There are no jellyfish at all," said Mia, sweeping her hand through the water. "It's so nice! You could just come and dip your toes in?"

Emily looked tempted. "Maybe later."

They got closer to the fishing boat. The two fishermen who were dragging the dinghy into the water were dressed in big yellow raincoats with the hoods pulled down over their faces.

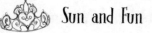

One fisherman was tall and the other was short. They were pushing the dinghy into the water but they seemed to be struggling with it.

"Can you two give us a hand?" called the short fisherman in a gruff, deep voice. "Could you give the boat a pull?"

Emily waited further back up the beach, away from the water. But Mia and

Charlotte waded deeper into the water
and helpfully pulled at the boat while
the shorter fisherman pushed. The taller
fisherman stood back and just watched.

"That's it!" said the shorter fisherman as
the boat bobbed into the water.

He stepped back, leaving Mia and
Charlotte holding the boat. They were up
to their chests in the sea now.

"Can you do us another favour, girls?
Climb in and we'll throw you our fishing
net," the shorter fishermen called.

Charlotte was already scrambling into
the boat and holding out her hand to Mia.

"That's right, my dears. You're so *very*
helpful," drawled the other fisherman.

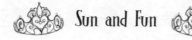

Hearing her speak, Mia realised the taller fisherman was a woman. She frowned. Her voice sounded familiar …

"Come on, Mia!" Charlotte said.

Mia climbed into the boat too. It bobbed up and down on the waves, floating further out to sea.

Charlotte called out to the fishermen, "We're ready! Throw us the net!"

The taller fisherman gave an amused snort. "No need. We've already caught what we wanted." She threw back her hood.

"Princess Poison!" gasped the girls as Princess Poison's hair tumbled around her shoulders. The shorter fisherman threw back his hood, too, and they saw that it was Hex.

Dolphin Adventure

He danced a jig on the sand, making his
tummy bounce up and down.

Princess Poison pointed her wand at the
dingy. "Have fun floating out to sea, girls!"

To Mia's horror, green light hit the boat
and pushed it out into deeper water.

"Hee hee hee! And there aren't any oars!

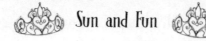

You can't paddle back to the beach!" Hex chortled meanly.

"So? We can swim!" Charlotte shouted. "You're not going to stop us!"

Mia glanced at Emily. She was watching from the beach, looking confused and worried. "Yeah, we'll just swim," she said.

"We'll see about that!" Princess Poison
pulled out her wand and called out:

**"Poisonous jellyfish come and float
All around this rowing boat!"**

There was a flash of green light and
suddenly lots of bright green jellyfish with
long stinging tentacles appeared. They
bobbed around the dinghy!

"Now what are we going to do?" Mia
gasped to Charlotte.

"You're done!" Hex gave another smug
laugh. "Done up like a kipper!"

"You can't even use magic to get back to
shore because, being good Secret Princesses,

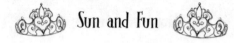

you know you must never use wishes to help yourselves," Princess Poison said.

A cruel smile crossed her face. "While you enjoy your little cruise, I'll make sure Emily's wish is well and truly ruined! Byeee!" She wiggled her fingers in a wave and then turned towards Emily, who was

still watching in
confusion. She
beckoned to her.

The little
girl went over
cautiously.

"Oh, dear,"
Princess Poison
said, bending down
to speak to her.
"It looks like your
little friends are stuck out there. You'd
better help them."

Mia grabbed Charlotte's arm. "If Emily
comes into the water, she'll get stung by a
jellyfish again!"

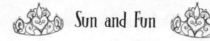
"That must be Princess Poison's plan," said Charlotte. Emily was hesitating by the edge of the water. "Go back, Emily! Don't come in!" Charlotte shouted. "There are—"

"Ssh! Don't tell her about the jellyfish," Mia whispered urgently. "It'll just make her even more scared of the sea."

"There's what?" Emily called anxiously.

"Umm ... really big waves," Charlotte said quickly.

"Oh, do go in and help your friends," Princess Poison urged. "Go on. Be brave. Just paddle into the water."

Emily put one foot in the water.

Princess Poison sniggered and walked off up the beach with Hex trotting beside her.

"No, Emily!" Charlotte cried. "Don't come in."

"But I want to help you!" Emily said, taking another step into the water.

Mia scanned the beach desperately, looking for help. How could they get rid of the jellyfish before they stung Emily? In the distance she saw some children playing chase on the beach. One girl was wearing a swimsuit with a shiny dolphin on it.

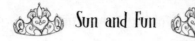

"I've got an idea!" she cried. "Remember the nature programme I told you about? The one where the dolphins chased the jellyfish away …"

Charlotte nodded.

"We can wish for dolphins," Mia said. "Emily loves them and maybe they'll chase the jellyfish away."

"It's worth a try!" Charlotte said, grabbing her pendant. "There isn't any time to lose. Look! The magic's almost gone!"

The pendants were only flickering with a very faint light now.

Mia and Charlotte fitted them quickly together. "I wish that there were lots of dolphins here!" said Charlotte.

For a moment, nothing seemed to have happened. "It hasn't worked," said Mia, her heart sinking as she looked at the jellyfish still bobbing around the boat. *What are we going to do?* she thought.

But just then Emily squealed in delight. "Dolphins!" she cried. She pointed behind the girls. "Look!"

CHAPTER SIX
A Dream Come True

Mia and Charlotte swung round. A pod of
ten grey bottlenose dolphins were swimming
towards them. The dolphins jumped joyfully
out of the waves, arcing over the water
before plunging back down.

"The wish worked!" Mia said, feeling
relief spread through her.

The dolphins raced towards the dingy.

Surrounding the jellyfish, they chased them all out to sea, far away from the beach.

Charlotte and Mia cheered in delight.

Then the dolphins turned and raced back. They swam around the dinghy, pushing it close to the shore. Bobbing their heads up above the water, the dolphins seemed to smile at the girls, their dark eyes shining.

Mia reached out and stroked their sleek heads. "Oh, you're gorgeous," she breathed. She'd never touched a real dolphin before. Its skin was warm and smooth.

"Wow … just, wow!" gasped Emily from the shore, the waves lapping around her feet. "I want to touch one."

"You'll have to come in the water, then," Charlotte called to her.

One of the dolphins swam as close to Emily as it could. It whistled encouragingly at her and waved its flipper.

"Go on, Emily! You'll be fine," said Mia. "The dolphin wants you to come in."

Emily fixed her gaze on the dolphin and carefully waded deeper into the water.

The dolphin waited for
her, grinning happily.
Finally, Emily
reached it.
She stroked
its head and
it nuzzled her
with its nose.
The water was
up to Emily's chest
but she didn't seem to notice. She patted
the dolphin and gave a happy sigh.

Two of the dolphins swam up to the side
of the dingy. They slapped their tails in the
water and whistled as they looked up at
Charlotte and Mia.

"It's like they're trying to tell us something," said Mia, curiously.

"I think they want us to get in the water too," said Charlotte.

She scrambled over the side of the boat. One dolphin swam up to her so that her hands were resting on its back. "Come on, Mia!" she urged.

Mia didn't need telling twice. She climbed over the side of the boat. As she slipped into the water, she felt another dolphin swim up beside her. She stroked its smooth body. "Hello," she murmured.

"Look at me!" cried Emily. Mia turned and saw that she was holding on to her dolphin's fin as it pulled her through the shallow water. Emily laughed in delight.

Mia and Charlotte's dolphins clicked and whistled excitedly.

"I think they want to give us a ride, too!" said Mia.

The girls took hold of their dolphins' fins and off they went! At first the dolphins swam slowly, but as the girls got used to the feeling they started to speed up. Soon they were all racing through the water, zooming this way and that.

"Wheeee!" Mia cried, as her dolphin streaked through the water. It was the most amazing feeling ever!

"Whoops!" Charlotte giggled as she lost hold of her dolphin's fin. The dolphin made

---

a clicking sound as if he was laughing, then circling round to pick her up again.

Then the girls and their dolphins played tag, swimming through the water to try and catch each other.

"Can't catch me!" cried Emily, diving under the water.

"Oh, yes, I can," laughed Charlotte, splashing after her.

"This is so much fun!" gasped Emily, when her dolphin towed her to the shallows where she could stand up. She hugged it. "The sea isn't scary at all … it's fun!"

Suddenly there was a magical tinkling noise and all ten dolphins leaped joyfully out of the sea and up into the air. They somersaulted, turned flips, plunged back into the water and leaped out again in an amazing acrobatic display.

"What's going on?" Emily said in astonishment.

Mia grinned. "Your wish has come true. You're not scared of the sea any more!"

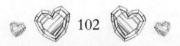

Emily beamed. "No, I'm not! Thanks to you and your magic!"

"No!" a harsh voice screeched.

Princess Poison had seen the dolphins' display and was stalking back down to the water. She looked scarier than ever as she stomped over the sand towards them.

"You silly girls!" she shrieked. "You'll never be Secret Princesses!"

"We're not silly!" Charlotte replied. "After all, we just made Emily's wish come true, and you didn't stop us!"

The dolphins surged forward in a line, protecting the girls. Princess Poison's face screwed up with rage. "I will next time!" she hissed. "I'll stop your meddling. I'll thwart any wishes you try to grant. I'll—"

The dolphins all turned round together and smacked their tails down hard on the water. Seaweed and water flew up in a big wave, drenching Princess Poison and Hex!

Princess Poison broke off from her rant with a shriek.

Charlotte giggled. "Looks
like you should have
kept your raincoat on,
Princess Poison!"
"Gah!" Princess
Poison spluttered,
as the dolphins
clapped their
flippers in
delight.

Spitting out a piece of seaweed, Princess
Poison stormed away.

"Wait for me!" Hex called. He pulled the
seaweed off his head and followed along
behind her.

Mia, Charlotte and Emily burst out
laughing. The dolphins swam around

them, clicking their tongues as if they were laughing too. The girls gave them a hug.

"That was brilliant," Charlotte said.

"Look! Mummy, Daddy and Sam are coming!" said Emily, seeing her family hurrying along the beach.

"Emily!" her mum cried. "You've been swimming!"

"I know! I'm not afraid of the water any more!" said Emily, running up to her. "It's the dolphins – they helped. And Mia and Charlotte too!"

"I've never seen so many dolphins," Emily's dad said, staring in astonishment.

"They're really friendly,' said Emily. "Come and swim with them."

Her brother and parents splashed into the water and the dolphins swam over to them.

Mia was about to go back in the water when Charlotte caught her arm. "Look over there. It's Alice!"

Alice was waving to them from the dry sand, wearing a red sparkly bikini and a short skirt. They hurried up the beach towards her.

"Well done, girls," she said, hugging them. "I've been watching you through the Magic Mirror. You did brilliantly."

"Did you see what Princess Poison did?" said Charlotte.

Alice nodded. "She's so awful. I'm glad you didn't let her beat you."

Mia squeezed Charlotte's hand. "We couldn't let her spoil Emily's wish."

Charlotte grinned. "No way. By the time they left, I think she and Hex were feeling quite *crabby*!"

Mia giggled. "They were, weren't they?

Serves them right for being so *shell-fish*!"

They both chuckled.

Alice's eyes glowed warmly. "Oh, I'm proud of you. And look what granting Emily's wish has done." She touched her wand to the sand. Suddenly, another sandcastle version of Wishing Star Palace appeared. Two of its turrets were now mended and gleaming with new tiles.

"It looks better," said Charlotte happily.

"Yes, much better," said Alice. She touched her wand to the sandcastle and it vanished into thin air. "Now, let me give you both something in return."

The girls grinned as Alice reached into her beach bag and brought out her wand.

With a smile,
Alice waved
her wand over
the girls.

There was
a flash of light
and suddenly
the girls were
wearing cute
beach outfits.
Better still, each of
their half-heart pendants glittered with a
second diamond.

"Yay!" said Charlotte, gazing down at the
new gem in her necklace.

"It's so lovely," sighed Mia.

"You just need two more to earn your jewelled tiaras," Alice told them happily. "Keep up the good work and it won't be long before you're full Secret Princesses." She put an arm around their shoulders and gave them both a hug. "But now it's nearly time for you both to go home. Do you want to go and say goodbye to Emily before you leave?"

Charlotte and Mia nodded and hurried back down to the sea, where Emily and her brother were having a splashing contest with the dolphins.

"We've got to go, Emily," called Mia.

Emily ran out of the water. "Thank you for helping me." She lowered her voice to

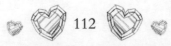

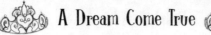
a whisper. "I'll
always believe
in magic from
now on."

"Have
a lovely
holiday!"
said Mia.

"I will,"
said Emily.
"And I'll never forget
what happened today, ever! Goodbye!"

She hugged them, and then Mia and
Charlotte ran back to Alice.

"Will Charlotte and I see each other
again soon?" Mia asked hopefully.

"Very soon," Alice promised. "After all, we need you to help us grant more wishes!"

Mia and Charlotte squeezed hands and then Alice waved her wand. Red sparkles flew out of the top and the next moment, Mia felt herself whizzing through the bright light. Round and round she spun until she came to a stop. She blinked. *Why was it dark?* she thought. Of course! She was in the tunnel of the aquarium – on her school trip.

Mia hurried into the next room. It was hard to believe that no one had noticed she'd been gone, but her class was trooping to the next display, just as they had been when she left.

"This way, everyone!" the guide was calling. "Now, in here you'll see lots of jellyfish!"

"Ew!"

"Yuck!"

"Jellyfish are scary!"

Mia hid her grin as she joined the back of the group. Jellyfish weren't that scary. At least, not compared to Princess Poison. But Mia knew that nothing was too scary when you had your best friend and Wish Magic on your side!

The End

Join Charlotte and Mia in their
next Secret Princesses adventure!

Read on for a sneak peek!

Starlight Sleepover

Sunlight shone through the treetops, casting
pretty stripes of light on the forest floor.
Charlotte couldn't believe how big the
giant redwood trees were. They towered
up into the sky, with massive green ferns
growing between them. *It feels magical
here,* Charlotte thought, looking round the
forest. *A unicorn could be watching me, or a
dragon!*

Up ahead of her, Liam, one of her little
brothers, called out, "Mum! Dad! Check out
this tree!"

The Williams family had only been living in California a few months, but Charlotte's brothers were already starting to sound American.

Charlotte ran to join Liam. "I bet we can't get our arms all the way around it, even if we all hold hands," she said. "Let's try."

Her mum, dad and Liam's twin, Harvey, hurried over and held hands, but the tree trunk was so thick they couldn't mange to make a circle around it.

"We're being watched," Mr Williams pointed out, as a chipmunk peered at them from one of the branches.

"They're so cute," said Charlotte, as the chipmunk scampered away.

"I hope we see a bear," said Harvey.

"If we do, I'll run!" said Liam.

"No, you mustn't," said Charlotte quickly. "If you run it'll chase you. You've got to make yourself seem big and make loads of noise to scare it away."

"How do you know?" asked Liam, impressed.

Charlotte grinned. "Mia, of course." Mia was her best friend who lived in England, where Charlotte and her family came from. Mia loved animals and was always sharing interesting facts about them. Charlotte sighed. "I wish she could see all the different animals here in California."

Her mum gave her shoulder a squeeze. "It

must feel like ages since you saw her."

Charlotte hid her smile. If only her mum knew! She and Mia had actually seen each other twice since she moved away. But no one else knew because it was a secret – a magical secret!

Charlotte felt a shiver of delight as she touched the gold pendant that hung around her neck. It was shaped like half a heart and had two diamonds embedded in it. Mia's pendant was the other half of the heart. When the necklaces glowed, they whisked Charlotte and Mia away to the most incredible, enchanted place in the whole world – Wishing Star Palace, home of the Secret Princesses!

If Charlotte and Mia completed their training, one day they would become princesses. And not just ordinary princesses, but Secret Princesses, who used magic to grant wishes. Sometimes Charlotte had to pinch herself to believe it was true!

A spark of light flew across the pendant. Charlotte frowned. Had she imagined it? But no! There was another! And another!

As her brothers scrambled over a fallen tree trunk, Charlotte ducked behind an enormous tree. The pendant began to sparkle and glow. Charlotte's tummy somersaulted with excitement. She was going to have an adventure!

She closed her fingers around the

pendant. No time would pass while she was away, so she knew her family wouldn't worry. "I wish I could see Mia!" she whispered.

WHOOSH! Charlotte felt herself spinning through the air in a tunnel of brilliant golden light. As soon as her feet hit solid ground she opened her eyes. Even though she had been there twice before, the entrance hall of Wishing Star Palace was so grand it made her gasp.

She glanced down and squealed with excitement. Her shorts and T-shirt had transformed into her beautiful pink princess dress with dark pink roses on the skirt, and she could feel her tiara sitting on her brown curls. "Yes!" she breathed, twirling around on the spot and making her pretty skirt spin out.

Read Starlight
Sleepover to find out
what happens next!

The Secret Princess Gallery

Alice

Job in the real world: Pop star

Her deepest wish: To play the world's biggest free concert

Her secret: She always sings in the shower

Sylvie

Job in the real world: Baker

Her deepest wish: To make her own wedding cake one day

Her secret: She sometimes licks the spoon clean!

Sophie

Job in the real world: Artist

Her deepest wish: That she could invent a new colour

Her secret: She's a bit untidy and sometimes forgets to clean her paintbrushes

Do you want to get to know more about the Secret Princesses? Here are some fun facts about them. Sssssh! Be sure not to tell anyone their secrets.

Ella

Job in the real world: Vet

Her deepest wish: That no more animals will become extinct

Her secret: Snakes give her the creeps

Anna

Job in the real world: Teacher

Her deepest wish: To travel to outer space

Her secret: She doesn't like giving out homework

Evie

Job in the real world: Trainee florist

Her deepest wish: To save the rainforests

Her secret: Some types of flowers make her sneeze

♥ FREE NECKLACE ♥

In every book of Secret Princesses series one: The Diamond Collection, there is a special Wish Token. Collect all four tokens to get an exclusive Best Friends necklace by

MONSOON
CHILDREN

for you and your best friend!

Simply fill in the form below, send it in with your four tokens and we'll send you your special necklaces.*

Send to: Secret Princesses Wish Token Offer, Hachette Children's Books Marketing Department, Carmelite House, 50 Victoria Embankment, London, EC4Y 0DZ

Closing Date: 31st December 2016

secretprincessesbooks.co.uk

---✂---

lease complete using capital letters (UK and Republic of Ireland sidents only)

RST NAME:

JRNAME:

ATE OF BIRTH: DD | MM | YYYY

DDRESS LINE 1:

DDRESS LINE 2:

DDRESS LINE 3:

OSTCODE:

ARENT OR GUARDIAN'S EMAIL ADDRESS:

I'd like to receive regular Secret Princesses email newsletters and information about other great Hachette Children's Group offers (I can unsubscribe at any time).

I'd like to receive regular Monsoon Children email newsletters (I can unsubscribe at any time).

Terms and Conditions apply. For full terms and conditions please go to secretprincessesbooks.co.uk/terms

1 Secret Princesses Wish Token

* 2000 necklace available while stocks last Terms and conditions apply.

Secret
PRINCESSES

What would you wish for?

Are you a Secret Princess?

Join the Secret Princesses Club at:

secretprincessesbooks.co.uk

Explore the magic of the
Secret Princesses and discover:

♥ Special competitions! ♥
♥ Exclusive content! ♥
♥ All the latest princess news! ♥

Open to UK and Republic of Ireland residents only
Please ask your parent/guardian for their permission to join

For full terms and conditions go to
secretprincessesbooks.co.uk/terms